Fireball Hall

Bedroom
and Bathroom

Living Room

Home

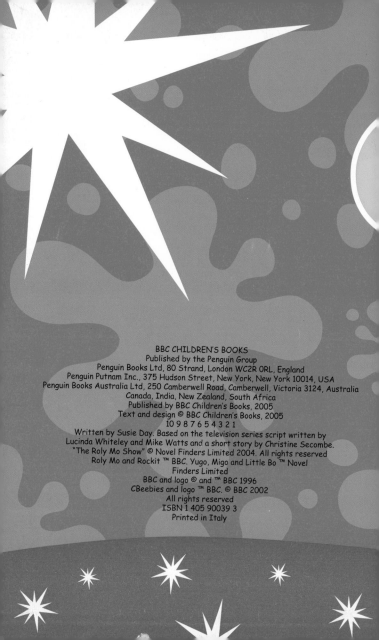

BBC CHILDREN'S BOOKS
Published by the Penguin Group
Penguin Books Ltd, 80 Strand, London WC2R 0RL, England
Penguin Putnam Inc., 375 Hudson Street, New York, New York 10014, USA
Penguin Books Australia Ltd, 250 Camberwell Road, Camberwell, Victoria 3124, Australia
Canada, India, New Zealand, South Africa
Published by BBC Children's Books, 2005
Text and design © BBC Children's Books, 2005
10 9 8 7 6 5 4 3 2 1
Written by Susie Day. Based on the television series script written by
Lucinda Whiteley and Mike Watts and a short story by Christine Secombe.
"The Roly Mo Show" © Novel Finders Limited 2004. All rights reserved
Roly Mo and Rockit ™ BBC. Yugo, Migo and Little Bo ™ Novel
Finders Limited
BBC and logo © and ™ BBC 1996
CBeebies and logo ™ BBC. © BBC 2002
All rights reserved
ISBN 1 405 90039 3
Printed in Italy

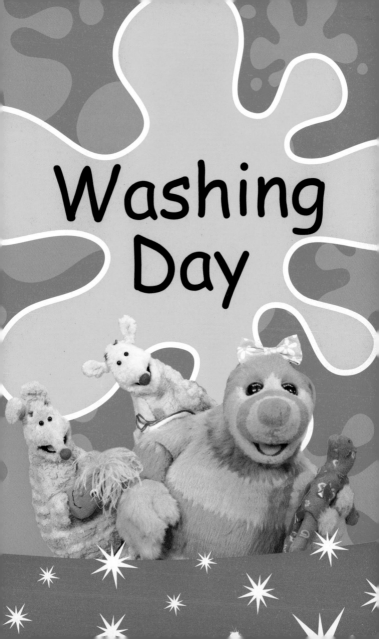

Washing Day

Roly Mo was in the kitchen
making tea when Little Bo
arrived, looking worried.
"What's the matter, Little Bo?"
said Roly.

"It's Floppy," sniffed Little Bo.
"She fell in the Purple Patch, and
now she's all grubby."

"That's easy enough to fix," said
Roly. "We'll give her a bath."

As Roly Mo went to run the bath,
up popped the Snoots.
"Yugo!"
"Migo!"
"We go...amigo!"
Little Bo showed them Floppy.

"Little Bo loves her Floppy, don't you, Bo?" said Yugo. "Just like I love my Snudge."

"And I love my Bibby," said Migo. "She's so cuddlicious!"

Yugo stared at Migo's Bibby.

"What's that?" he said, pointing at a dribbly yellow blob.

"Oh, that's just yesterday's tea," said Migo.

"And that one?"

"I'm not sure," said Migo, sniffing a splodge of purple. "It might be rhubarb jam."

"Migo," said Yugo, seriously. "Bibby needs a wash."

"Nooooo!" cried Migo. "No wash for Bibby!"

Roly Mo heard the noise and came back to see what all the fuss was about.

"Bibby's dirty, Uncle Roly," said Little Bo. "Just like Floppy!"

"Bibby could have a bath, just like Floppy," suggested Yugo.

Migo looked horrified. "No she couldn't!"

"Yes she could!" said Yugo.

"Couldn't!"

"Could!"

"Couldn't couldn't couldn't!"

"Ahem!" said Roly Mo. "Now then,
Yugo, why don't you help Little Bo
wash Floppy?"
Migo looked up at Roly, and
clutched Bibby very tightly.

"And why don't you sit down in the living room, Migo," said Roly, "and I'll find us a story to read."

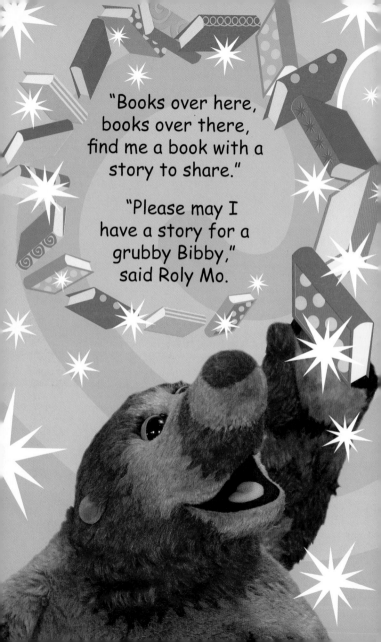

"Books over here,
books over there,
find me a book with a
story to share."

"Please may I
have a story for a
grubby Bibby,"
said Roly Mo.

Tea for
Two

Josh didn't understand why his mum was always telling him to wash his hands.

One afternoon, Josh decided to have a tea party with Teddy. He didn't notice that his Auntie Lou was fast asleep in the big armchair.

"Time for a tea party, Teddy," said Josh. "We've got cups, and plates, and shiny teaspoons."

"Those teaspoons aren't shiny!" said a voice.

Josh sat back in amazement. Who was talking to him? Could it be...Teddy?

"And those cups and plates are grubby, too!" said the voice.

"I'll go and wash them, Teddy," said Josh.
He gave everything a good scrub.
Afterwards, the cups and plates and
teaspoons were lovely and clean and shiny.

When Josh came back, he spotted Auntie
Lou in the armchair. That's where the voice
had come from!

"Time for tea, Teddy," said Josh. "Would
you like some tea too, Auntie Lou?"

Auntie Lou yawned, pretending to wake up.
Then she saw Josh laughing, and chuckled.

"Yes please," she said. "But first, I think
I'd better wash my hands!"

The End

"I liked that story," said Migo.
"It was all about tea!"
"And it was about something else
too, wasn't it?" said Roly.

"Yes," said Migo. "Everything was all clean and shiny when Josh had washed it."

He sat quietly for a moment.

"You know, Roly, maybe washing something isn't so bad after all."

In the bathroom, Little Bo had
wrapped Floppy up in a fluffy green
towel. Floppy was back to her old
pink self.

Then Little Bo noticed a curious
snooter peeping over the edge of
the bath.

"Look how clean Floppy is, Migo!"
she said.

Migo looked.

"The bath's still warm," Yugo added.

Migo tested the water with the tip
of his snooter. It was warm.

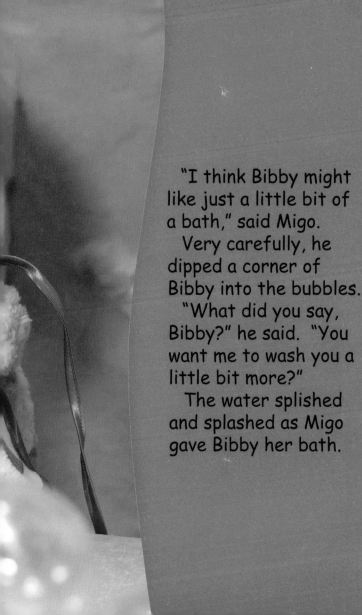

"I think Bibby might like just a little bit of a bath," said Migo.

Very carefully, he dipped a corner of Bibby into the bubbles.

"What did you say, Bibby?" he said. "You want me to wash you a little bit more?"

The water splished and splashed as Migo gave Bibby her bath.

When Roly Mo came in, Bibby and Floppy were both clean and dry.

"Is that a clean Bibby I can smell?" said Roly Mo.

"One clean Bibby!" said Migo proudly.

Yugo's snooter twitched. "I can smell tea too!"

"Yummity yum!" cried Migo. "Come on, Bibby, let's get you all grubby again!"

The End

Entrance H[

Library

Kitchen

Roly M